D0892604

This Topsy and Tim
book belongs to

_____

Topsy + Tim

meet the
ambulance crew

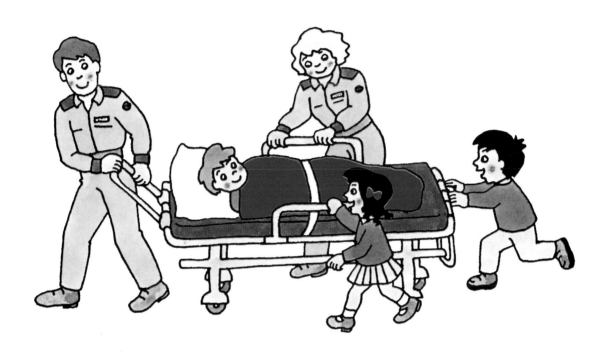

Jean and Gareth Adamson

Ladybird

All Ladybird books are available at most bookshops, supermarkets
and newsagents, or can be ordered direct from:
Ladybird Postal Sales PO Box 133 Paignton TQ3 2YP England
Telephone: (+44) 01803 554761   *Fax:* (+44) 01803 663394

A catalogue record for this book is available from the British Library

Published by Ladybird Books Ltd
A subsidiary of the Penguin Group
A Pearson Company

When Topsy and Tim arrived at school,
they saw a big, white ambulance standing
in the school playground.
'Oh dear,' said Mummy. 'I hope there
hasn't been an accident.'
'It's all right Mum,' said Tim. 'We're
going to learn all about the Ambulance
Service today. That's why the ambulance
is here.'

The twins ran to tell their teacher that the ambulance had arrived and saw two strangers in their classroom. Topsy and Tim guessed they were the ambulance crew.

'Dave and Nicky have come to
tell us all about their work,' said
Miss Terry. 'Dave is a Paramedic and
Nicky is an Ambulance Technician.
They are trained to help people, a bit like
doctors and nurses.'

Everyone sat down to listen to Dave
and Nicky tell them about the
Ambulance Service.
'Let's start at the beginning,' said
Dave. 'I want one of you children
to pretend to have an accident.'

Andy Anderson pretended to fall off
a chair. 'OW, OW, OW!' he cried.
'Andy's hurt! He's broken his leg,'
said Topsy.
'And his arm,' said Tim.
'Andy needs to get to hospital quickly,'
said Nicky. 'Does anyone know how to
phone for an ambulance?'

'I do,' said Louise Lewis. 'My mummy taught me.' Louise rang 999 on the toy telephone.
'Hello,' she said. 'Please send an ambulance to Hatcham School. Andy has fallen off a chair and broken his leg and his arm.'

'Ambulance Control tells us where
to go,' said Dave, 'so we can get there
as quickly as possible.'
He knelt down and felt Andy's leg.
'This leg is broken,' he said.
'His arm is broken too.
We need splints and a stretcher.'
Nicky hurried out to the ambulance
to get them.

'If Andy's leg and arm are hurt very badly
we would let him breathe some special gas
to stop the pain,' said Technician Nicky.
She took a little mask out of a blue bag
and showed Andy how to put it on.

Paramedic Dave put a splint on
Andy's leg and a sling on his arm.
'These will keep Andy's arm and leg
steady and comfortable on the way
to hospital,' explained Dave.

Nicky and Dave tucked Andy up
on the stretcher and wheeled him
out to the ambulance. Miss Terry
and all the children followed and
watched them lift the stretcher
into the ambulance. Andy looked
very comfortable.

'You can all come and look inside the ambulance,' called Dave, 'but there isn't room for everyone at once.' Miss Terry divided the class into two groups. The first group climbed the ambulance steps and went inside.

Topsy and Tim were in the second group, so they had to wait outside. They ran around the playground shouting 'Nee-nor, nee-nor, nee-nor.' 'Steady, children,' said Miss Terry. 'We're ambulances hurrying to an accident,' said Topsy.

At last the first group came out.
Andy came out too. Now it was the
turn of Topsy and Tim's group to go
into the ambulance. They climbed
up the big steps and went in.

The ambulance was full of all sorts
of interesting things.
'This special blue Trauma light is
for patients who can't look at bright
lights,' said Dave. 'It shows up bruises
too.' Topsy had a bruise on her leg.
The blue light showed it up well.

There were cupboards full of useful
things all around the ambulance.
Kerry tried on an oxygen mask.
A little red ball in a tube measured
the oxygen she was breathing.

'We all need oxygen to stay alive,'
said Nicky. 'There is plenty in the air,
but sometimes, when people are ill,
they need extra.'
Vinda and Tony took turns to measure
their oxygen levels by putting a special
clip on their fingers. A screen
told them how much they had.

Tim saw another screen.
'Is that a TV?' he asked.
'No,' said Dave. 'It's a Heart Monitor.
It shows a picture of your heartbeat.
If you were very ill and your heart
stopped beating we would try
to start it again.'

Nicky turned a Suction Unit on and
Stevie felt it suck at his hand.
'This is to stop people choking,' said
Nicky. 'It's like the sucking tube the
dentist puts in your mouth.'

Two brightly coloured jackets were hanging up behind the front seats. 'We wear these when we go to road accidents, so that the traffic can see us easily,' said Dave. Topsy and Tim tried the yellow jackets on.
'They're a bit big!' said Topsy.

Suddenly a voice said, 'Control
to Nicky and Dave. I have an
emergency for you.' It was the
Ambulance Controller speaking on
the radio.
'Hello, Control,' said Dave into the
mike. 'We will be on our way
as quickly as possible.'

Miss Terry helped the children
out of the ambulance. Topsy
and Tim were the last to leave.
'Are you going to turn on the siren
and flashing lights?' asked Tim.
'Would you and Topsy like to do
it for us?' asked Nicky.
'Yes please,' said Topsy and Tim.
Nicky let Topsy press the button
for the flashing lights. Tim pressed
the button for the siren.

The ambulance drove out of the school playground with blue lights flashing and siren sounding. It was very noisy. The children shouted 'THANK YOU!' and waved goodbye.
'I'm going to be a Paramedic and help people when I grow up,' said Topsy.
'Me, too,' said Tim.